This book is for

BABYMOON

Hayley Barrett

illustrated by Juana Martinez-Neal

WALKER BOOKS
AND SUBSIDIARIES

LONDON • BOSTON • SYDNEY • AUCKLAND

The house is hushed. The lights are low.
We're basking in a newborn glow.

The note we post says SEE YOU SOON.

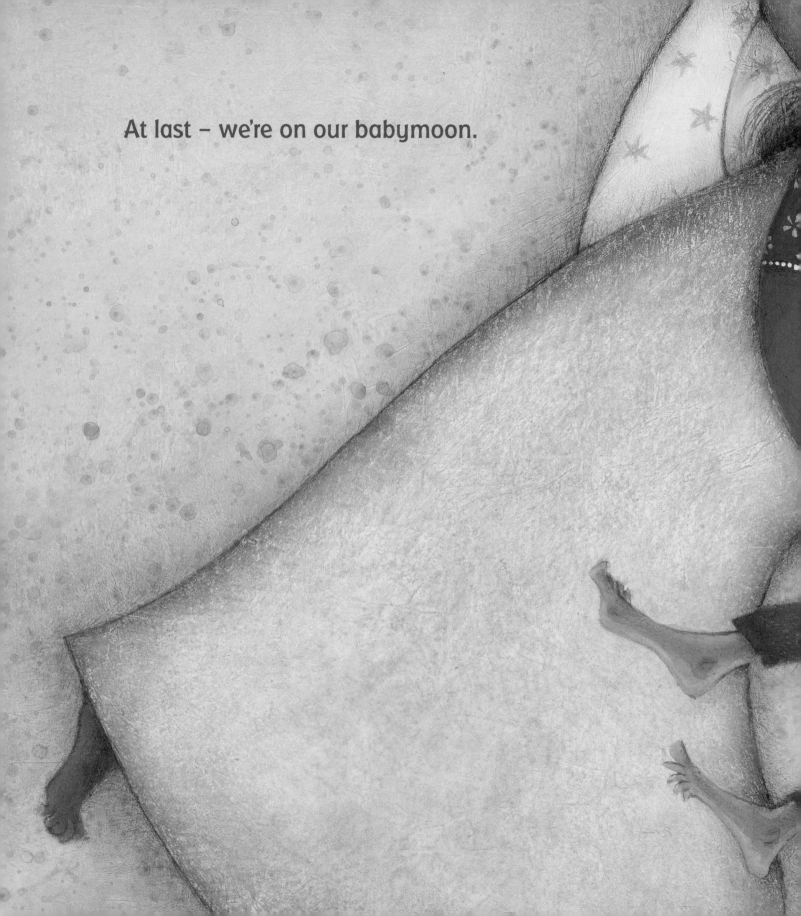

At last – we're on our babymoon.

A mellow morning, sunny naps –
we stroll about in matching caps.

We're reading stories, playing games.
We're getting used to brand-new names.

Endearing sneezes. Solemn eyes.
Delighting in each small surprise.

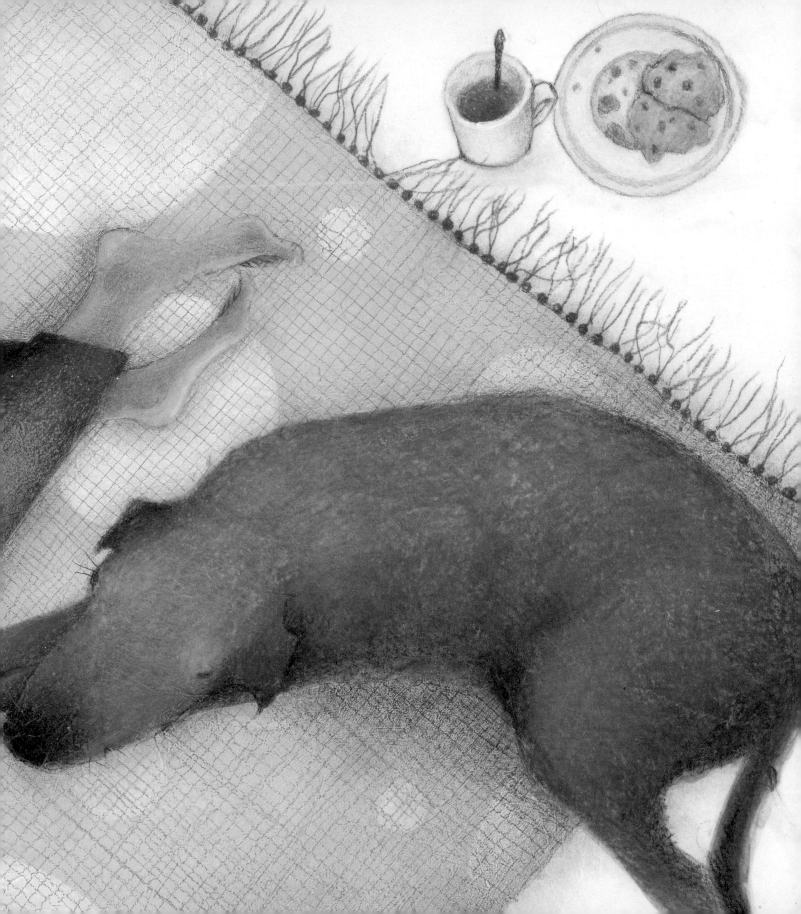

A tender dance of give-and-take.
We share a tiny *birth day* cake.

A sweet, secluded afternoon –
this restful time, our babymoon.

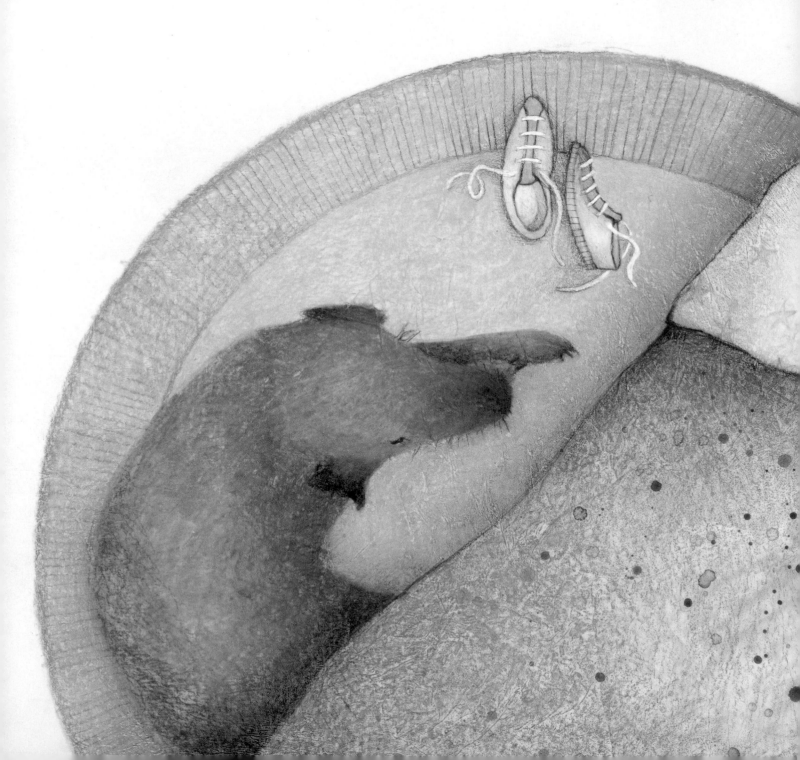

Soothing water and warm embrace
of tentative and awkward grace.

Here together. So much to learn.
We muddle through each new concern.

We're reassuring, building trust –
believing that we'll soon adjust.

Our long-awaited dream – is you.
Amazed at all we thought we knew.

Drowsy contentment. Cool night air.
We're cuddled in the rocking chair.

Familiar lullabies to croon.
This gentle time, our babymoon.

Then morning beckons, rosy dawn –
now greeted with a tiny yawn.

We'll invite the world in soon,
but for now – we're on our babymoon.

For my parents, Jean and Warren Dalton,
who welcomed five children with gentleness and respect.
And for the late anthropologist Sheila Kitzinger, MBE,
who coined the word "babymoon" to encourage new families
to take time to rest, learn, and fall in love.
H. B.

To all new parents
J. M.-N.

First published 2019 by Walker Books Ltd
87 Vauxhall Walk, London SE11 5HJ

2 4 6 8 10 9 7 5 3 1

Text © 2019 Hayley Barrett
Illustrations © 2019 Juana Martinez-Neal

The right of Hayley Barrett and Juana Martinez-Neal to be identified as the author and illustrator respectively of this work
has been asserted by them in accordance with the Copyright, Designs and Patents Act 1988

This book has been typeset in Badger

Printed in China

British Library Cataloguing in Publication Data: a catalogue record for this book is available from the British Library

ISBN 978-1-4063-8736-0

www.walker.co.uk